Creepy-Crawly BIRTHDAY

HAROLD & CHESTER

IN

Creepy-Crawly
BIRTHDAY

JAMES HOWE

Illustrated by

LESLIE MORRILL

Morrow Junior Books / New York

This one is for
BENJAMIN AND THOMAS

Text copyright © 1991 by James Howe
Illustrations copyright © 1991 by Leslie Morrill
All rights reserved.
No part of this book may be reproduced or utilized
in any form or by any means, electronic or mechanical,
including photocopying, recording or by any information
storage and retrieval system,
without permission in writing from the Publisher.
Inquiries should be addressed to
William Morrow and Company, Inc.,
1350 Avenue of the Americas,
New York, NY 10019.

Printed in the United States of America.
1 2 3 4 5 6 7 8 9 10

Library of Congress Cataloging-in-Publication Data
Howe, James, 1946–
Creepy-crawly birthday / James Howe ; illustrated by
Leslie Morrill.
p.   cm.
Summary: The animals in the Monroe household fear
they are about to be replaced when
seven suitcases, apparently containing new pets,
arrive on Toby's birthday.
ISBN 0-688-09687-5. —ISBN 0-688-09688-3 (lib. bdg.)
[1. Dogs—Fiction.   2. Cats—Fiction.   3. Birthdays—Fiction.]
I. Morrill, Leslie H., ill.   II. Title.   III. Title: Creepy-crawly birthday.
PZ7.H83727Hap 1991
[E]—dc20   90-35370   CIP   AC

NOTE

The type of birthday-party entertainment presented in this book is not uncommon. To the best of the author's knowledge, animal handlers are trained and experienced and take great care to assure that the animals are in no way harmed or mistreated. While such forms of entertainment are meant to be enjoyed, their purpose is largely educational.

A Note to the Reader

The story you are about to read is told by a dog. But Harold is no ordinary dog. He has written other books about his family, the Monroes, and about his friends—Chester, a cat; Howie, a dachshund puppy; and Bunnicula, a most unusual rabbit.

Harold sent this story to me, along with a note that read:

Birthday parties are usually a lot of fun—even for us pets. There are refreshments and games and surprises. But at Toby's last birthday party, Chester, Howie, and I got one surprise too many. We were having a great time when all of a sudden we found ourselves alone in the basement and . . .

Well, I'll let you find out for yourself what happened next. All I can tell you is that Toby didn't have just a happy *birthday; he had a creepy-crawly, slithery, slimy, hoppy birthday, too!*

I couldn't help wondering what Harold meant. By the time I found out, I'd had almost as much fun as if I'd gone to Toby's party myself. And I'd learned something, too: The next time I'm invited to a birthday party, before I say yes, I'm going to find out who else—or *what* else—is going to be there.

—THE EDITOR

Toby's birthday was here at last. I had been waiting for weeks.

"Toby has the *best* birthday parties," I said to Chester. "Remember last year?"

Chester licked his whiskers. "Mrs. Monroe left a gallon of ice cream out on the kitchen table," he said dreamily.

"If we hadn't come along," said Howie, "that ice cream would have melted all over the place and made a terrible mess."

We all glanced toward the kitchen door, but decided it was too early for ice cream.

So we joined the party instead.

I soon noticed that Toby was missing and went to investigate.
And that's when I heard the words that started all the trouble.

"I know you're eager to show everyone your special birthday present," Mrs. Monroe was saying to Toby. "How about right before the cake?"

"Great," Toby said. "But remember: It's a secret. I don't even want Harold and Chester and Howie to know."

"My lips are sealed," Mrs. Monroe said. "Now what do you say we get back to our guests?"

I scampered out of the way before the door opened and they caught me listening.

"Chester! Howie!" I cried. "Toby has a special birthday present. And he's keeping it secret—even from *us*."

"But Toby doesn't keep secrets from us," Howie said.

Chester raised an eyebrow. "Well, I just happen to know where all of Toby's presents are."

"What are we waiting for?" Howie yipped. "Let's go!"

Chester led the way to Mr. Monroe's study.

"How do we know which one is the special present?" I wondered aloud.

"And why doesn't Toby want us to know about it?" Howie asked.

"Well," said Chester, "there's one way to find out the answer to both your questions."

"Nothing suspicious here," I said.

"I haven't found anything, either," said Howie.

Chester didn't say a word, but I noticed that his tail was twitching as he peered into the darkened corner of the room. "What are *those*?" he asked in a low voice.

"Suitcases," I said. "Could they be Toby's special present? What would an eight-year-old want with seven suitcases?"

"Ah, but those are no *ordinary* suitcases," said Chester.

I groaned. Chester's imagination gets the better of him sometimes. I mean, he honestly believes the family's pet rabbit, Bunnicula, is a vampire. "Let me guess," I said. "These are really aliens in disguise, right? Suitcases from outer space. Unidentified Flying Overnight Bags."

I was beginning to enjoy myself when one of the suitcases started to inch its way toward us.

"Living luggage!" Howie cried.

"Precisely," said Chester. "Don't you see? Don't you *smell,* at least? There are *animals* inside those cases."

It was then that I noticed the holes in the sides. And the eyes staring out of them.

There *were* animals in there.

What were animals doing in suitcases in Mr. Monroe's study?

"Oh, no!" someone cried. I looked up. It was Toby's brother, Pete. "You guys are *not* supposed to be in this room. Mom!"

Mrs. Monroe came running. "Oh, dear," she said when she saw us. "I'm sorry, fellas, but you can't be here. Pete, will you take care of them, please?"

The next thing we knew we were in the cellar.

"Look!" Howie gasped.

There on Mr. Monroe's workbench was Bunnicula, sound asleep in his cage.

"What's *he* doing here?" Howie asked. Bunnicula's cage is always kept in the living room.

Chester's eyes narrowed to little slits. "Toby didn't want us to know about his 'special birthday present,'" he murmured. "Meanwhile, there are seven strange animals in Mr. Monroe's study. And *we're* in the basement. Does any of this suggest anything, Harold?"

"Not really," I said. I hate it when Chester asks me to think.

"Pets!" Chester shouted. "The Monroes are giving Toby *seven new pets* for his birthday!"

"But why would they do that?" Howie whimpered. "Aren't *we* enough?"

Chester snorted. "Apparently not," he said. "Well, I won't stand for it!"

"Me, either!" I said.

"Me, either!" said Howie. And he promptly sat down.

"Follow me!" Chester ordered.

Luckily for us, the cellar door wasn't locked and there was no one
in the kitchen.

We moved swiftly and quietly down the back hall, past the
living room, where the party was going full blast...

to the door of the study.

"What's your plan?" I whispered to Chester.

"We're going to let them loose."

"*What?*"

"They're strange animals in a strange place," Chester explained. "Before you know it, they'll be running around, acting crazy. All we have to do is sit quietly on the sidelines: perfect examples of perfect pets."

"I like your thinking," I told Chester.

I pushed the door open, walked over to the suitcases, and quickly worked the latches loose. Fortunately, they were old and easy to budge.

"Out, out!" I woofed.

But no one moved. The suitcases were so still, I began to wonder if Chester had only imagined they were filled with animals.

But there *was* that peculiar odor. . . .

And then one of the suitcases started to wiggle and shake.
And then another. And another. And out THEY came.

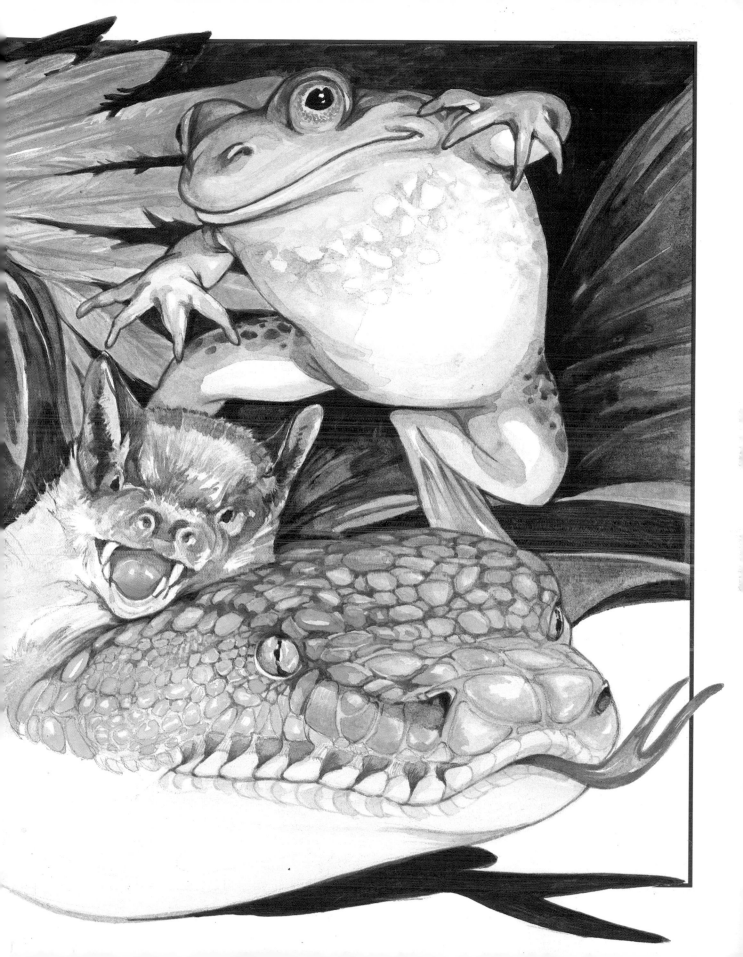

Howie went nuts immediately. I gave it a good six seconds before losing my cool.

"*Let me out of here!*" I barked.

Chester and I got tangled in each other's legs as we dashed out the door and into the living room...

where Howie had already had an encounter with Toby's birthday cake.

"Hey, watch it!"

"Mom, how did *they* get in here?"

"They're ruining my party!"

"Well, Chester," I said, "I think we've blown it as perfect pets."

No sooner had Mrs. Monroe grabbed Howie than there was a
piercing scream.

"Snakes!" someone was shouting.

"Rats!" cried someone else. "Creepy-crawlies everywhere! What
kind of party *is* this?"

There was a stampede to the door...

but a man blocked the way.

"Mrs. Monroe, how did all my animals get loose?" the man asked.

"I'm so sorry, Mr. Hu," said Mrs. Monroe. "We'll find them all, won't we, boys and girls?"

Chester, Howie, and I were rather rudely escorted out the door as the birthday party turned into a search party.

There at the curb sat a van. I read aloud the sign on its side: "Hu's Zoo."

"Who's who?" said Howie. "Well, I'm Howie and you're—"

I ignored Howie and went on reading. "Unusual Animals for All Occasions—Birthday Parties My Specialty." I turned to Chester. "Nice going," I said.

Chester looked up at the sky. "Looks like we might be in for a little rain," he commented.

We sneaked back into the house to watch Mr. Hu's show.

"Notice how the hedgehog rolls up into a little ball when you hold him," Mr. Hu said as he handed the little fellow to Toby.

"Wow," Toby said, "he feels like a hairbrush!"

"Who would like to touch the iguana?" Mr. Hu asked.

"This is the weirdest birthday entertainment I ever saw," Chester whispered. "Whatever happened to clowns?"

"I think it's interesting," I told Chester.

"Me, too," said Howie.

Pretty soon, Mr. Hu had all his animals out of their suitcases again. But, if my figuring was right, there should have been seven animals altogether. I counted only six.

One was missing.

"I'm sure it will turn up sooner or later," Mrs. Monroe was saying to Mr. Hu, as she let us join the party again. The animals were back in their cases.

"I'm sorry, you guys," Toby said to us. "I should have told you before. Mr. Hu has a rule: No pets in the same room with his animals. I guess you never know when a boa constrictor is going to want a little between-meals snack."

I looked into Toby's eyes to see if he was joking.

"If the *animals* aren't Toby's special present," Howie whispered, "what is?"

Toby must have been reading Howie's mind.

"Come on, follow me," he said to us. "I have a surprise for you."

"It's a clubhouse!" Toby shouted. "Isn't it great?"

So *this* was Toby's special birthday present.

"Look, it's even got special places just for us," I said to Howie and Chester. "That must have been why Toby was keeping it secret—he wanted to surprise us. I can't believe we ever thought he would want any other pets."

"Yeah," said Howie. "Whose idea was that, anyway?"

Chester didn't answer. He was busy licking his tail, which is a cat's way of trying to act cool when he knows he's made a total fool of himself.

Back inside, we all sang "Happy Birthday" to Toby. Mr. Hu had gone on to another party. He asked the Monroes to call him as soon as they spotted his missing animal. They promised they would.

Toby's party was so much fun, I had the feeling the missing animal might have been hiding from Mr. Hu. "Maybe," I told Chester, "he just wanted to hang around for a while and have some fun, too."

Chester looked at me and shook his head. "Really, Harold," he said, "that's the battiest thing I ever heard."

E

Howe, James

Creepy-crawly birthday

13.88